Jake and The Lake

written by
Christine Patton

illustrated by
Catherine Suvorova

For my Jeff at his lake...

C.P.

STORYBOOK GENIUS PUBLISHING
sbgpublishing.com

Book Design by yipjar.com

On one sunny morning,
a boy named Jake
woke up with a
question about
the lake!

"How deep is the lake? Can it be measured in feet?"
Jake wondered out loud as he smelled a sweet treat!

From the kitchen his mother yelled,

"JAKE, PLEASE BE HOME BY ONE! THAT IS WHEN THE CAKE WILL BE COOKED, ICED AND DONE!"

He dashed for the door and threw on his shoes.
"I must measure the lake! There is no time to lose!"

Jake ran fast,
quick as a wink!

He nearly passed
a sunbathing mink!

"Slow down, friend. Why are you running so quick,
and what are you doing with that very big stick?"
asked the mink.

"My name is Jake and there's a job I must do.
If you follow me now, you can come, too."

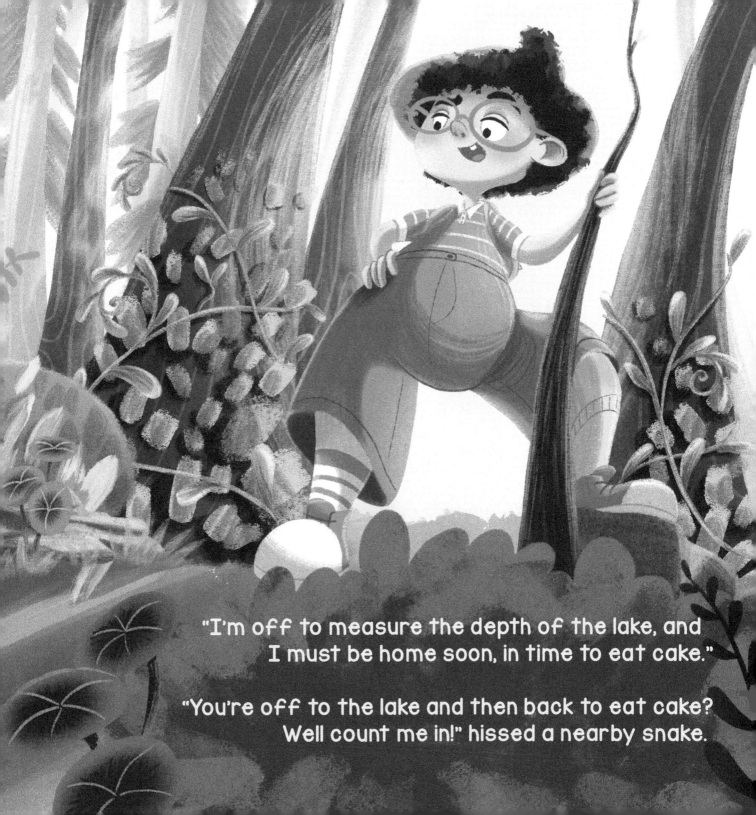

"I'm off to measure the depth of the lake, and
I must be home soon, in time to eat cake."

"You're off to the lake and then back to eat cake?
Well count me in!" hissed a nearby snake.

So the three new friends marched on toward the lake—Mink, Snake and their BOLD LEADER JAKE!

Before they knew it, they were almost there!
But suddenly—they were stopped by a curious hare!

What is this all about? Why the fuss you three make?
Why are you marching down to the lake?" asked the hare.

"The water is deep, but no one knows, just how deep the old lake goes. We're going to measure, and without a doubt, we will answer the question, and finally find out!" hissed the Snake.

"Oh, how exciting! It sounds truly fun! Do you have room for me? I am just one!" asked the Hare.

The new friends agreed.
They had room for Hare!

Then off they hurried.
Jake had no time to spare!

They made it to the dock and
Jake stepped up without fear...

...as the answer to his
question was so very near!

From somewhere in the distance a voice called out loudly.

"THE CAKE IS READY!"
called Jake's mom, proudly.

The four new friends knew what they must do!

They would take a break to celebrate friendships anew!

Someday soon...they would return
and the depth of the lake they would learn.

But for now, they would share laughs and some cake, all glad to have met Jake at the lake!

CPSIA information can be obtained
at www.ICGtesting.com
Printed in the USA
BVHW021627010721
610980BV00020B/1835